The Bungalo Boys

by John Bianchi

"LAST OF THE TREE RANCHERS!"

It is just after dawn in Beaver Valley, and as the sun climbs into the sky, the Bungalo Boys prepare for another busy day out on the range.

Curly combs his hair.　　　　　Johnny-Bob flosses his teeth.

Rufus stacks the breakfast dishes as Little Shorty washes up.
Ma Bungalo keeps a close eye on her boys.

There is no end to the list of the Bungalo Boys' chores.

The stock has to be watered and saddled.

Even Little Shorty lends a hand.

Moving the main herd is no problem. The Bungalo Boys are a seasoned bunch of tree ranchers, the last of a rare breed.

Johnny-Bob, a veteran ranch hand, is quick to rope in a nervous stray.
Little Shorty still has not learned all the ropes.

It's branding time, and the boys find that
putting the famous "double B" on a big one can
be a hot, tough job.

Little Shorty is distracted for just a second and accidentally puts the famous "double B" on the seat of Curly's pants.

Luckily, it's chow time, and the Bungalo Boys turn their attention to a hearty lunch. Ma brings all the fixin's in the chuck wagon, and under her direction, the Boys prepare their own meal. Ma Bungalo has vowed that her boys won't grow up to be helpless men.

Forgetting his manners, Little Shorty eats the last of the pickles — Curly's favourite treat.

"The Triple"

Tongue-twisting
saddle stand

Single-handed
limb cling

Backwood
head glide

After lunch, Johnny-Bob shows his brothers some pretty fancy riding. A rodeo champion, Johnny-Bob has mastered the difficult "Triple."

"Careful, Johnny-Bob," shouts Ma. "Don't fall off your tree."

She cautions that only experienced riders should attempt these tricks.

Little Shorty is not allowed.

Later, out on the south forty, the Boys make an unpleasant discovery—rustlers!

"I think I know who's behind this," says Rufus. This time, there is no doubt.

"Yup," says Curly, "looks like the work of the Beaver Gang."

The Beavers have been rustling trees in the valley for a long time, and the Bungalo Boys agree they must find their stock while the trail is fresh.

Eager to help, Little Shorty puts the Bungalos' wonder dog "Projectile" on the scent.

In no time, Projectile has brought the Boys within sight of their quarry.

"There they are, Boys!" shouts Johnny-Bob loudly. He is usually the quiet one.

Little Shorty is quick to give chase.

The Boys spur their mounts into a frenzied gallop and swoop down on the flat-tailed varmints.

The Beavers panic and make a run for it, but the thundering Bungalo Boys rain on their parade.

Johnny-Bob uses his famous lariat.

Curly chooses a classic tail tackle.

Little Shorty's method is not as smooth.
"Good work," says Rufus. "I'll take it from here."

The Beavers are quickly subdued. But Little Shorty has skinned his knee quite badly. Rufus gets the first-aid kit from his saddlebag while Projectile offers a chocolate-chip dog cookie.

Curly, a budding tree surgeon, does what he can for the recovered stock—most have been badly mistreated. He believes that the Beavers will never change.

"They are nothing but animals," he snorts.

Johnny-Bob — an amateur artist — takes some time to do pencil sketches of the captured criminals. Someday, he hopes to find a publisher for his work.

Night is falling, and the Boys decide to make camp. After supper, Rufus entertains with a tune on his mouth organ. It is hard to resist a Rufus Bungalo harmonica riff, and even the Beavers find themselves singing along.

Little Shorty is chosen to clean up while his brothers relax.

"Ma would be proud of you," says Curly.

When it's time for the Boys to turn in, Little
Shorty is chosen to stand guard over the Beaver
Gang.

"It will help you learn responsibility," his
brothers assure him.

The Bungalo Boys love camping out under the
stars and soon fall asleep.

Bored with his task, Little Shorty has slipped
away for a quick moonlight ride on Curly's prize
thoroughbred, Scotchy. He is sure the Beavers
won't even notice he is gone.

Proud of his role in the day's adventure, Little Shorty can't wait until his brothers tell Ma Bungalo how helpful he has been. Gazing up at the moon, he hums a favourite tree-ranching tune:

> "Yippie tie-yie yay,
> get along little sapling.
> The beavers are captured
> And will be chewing no more . . ."

Bungalo Boys II

By John Bianchi

Bushmen Brouhaha

An orange glow from the morning sun burns the mist off the African savannah. High overhead in a small plane, the **Bungalo Boys** prepare to drop into the magic and mystery of the Serengeti.

On board the plane, the Bungalo Boys
check their equipment one last time.

Curly makes sure his hair tonic is
tightly capped. Johnny-Bob inspects
his supply of tooth-care products. Ma
Bungalo, the plane's pilot, helps Rufus
secure the lid on a crate of supplies.

After playing hide-and-seek in the parachute,
Little Shorty hastily repacks it in preparation for
the big jump.

Rather than land the noisy plane, the boys
have decided to hit the silk . . .

. . . so as not to disrupt the peaceful lives of the animals below.

Once on the ground, the Bungalo Boys
establish base camp Bravo Bravo.
  During breakfast, Rufus wonders if they have
pitched their tent too close to one of the
Serengeti's many migration routes.

Later that morning, the wily Bungalo Boys approach some local bushmen. Though Johnny-Bob does not recognize their dialect, he is able to use Universal Bungalo Sign Language to engage them for the expedition.

Some Universal Bungalo Sign Language:

"Bunny Rabbit"

"Walk"

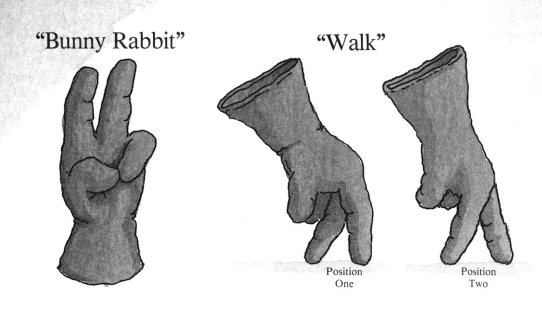

Position One

Position Two

"Hop"

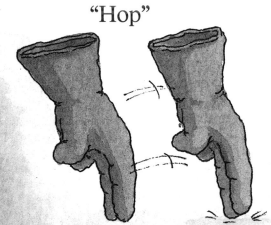

Position One

Position Two

"Do you have a spare banana?"

The bushmen help the boys track and capture an elusive Tanzanian elephant tree. In no time, the big-game tree ranchers have tamed the magnificent beast.

"Let's call her Buffy!" suggests Johnny-Bob.

With Projectile the wonder dog bounding ahead and the Bungalo Boys high atop Buffy the Tanzanian elephant tree, the Serengeti expedition is finally under way.

The bushmen follow closely behind, carrying the boys' equipment and singing rhythmic native songs. Already, Little Shorty is hungry.

The Bungalo Boys are gifted naturalists. They encounter many exotic animals and skillfully record their findings while leaving the beauty of the Serengti virtually undisturbed.

Little Shorty is left in charge of the bushmen. Within minutes, they are surrounded by a tribe of hungry blue-nosed baboons intent on feasting upon the bushmen's berries.

"What now, Little Bwana?" signs the head bushman nervously.

Little Shorty panics! In a mindless attempt to drive the baboons away, he lights a nearby branch.

"LITTLE BWANA GOT BANANA FOR BRAIN!!!" shouts the head bushman. "YOU TORCH BROTHER SABU! NOW WHOLE SAVANNAH GO UP IN SMOKE!!!"

The ensuing hubbub alerts the ever vigilant Bungalo Boys.

"Jumpin' Jack Pines!" shouts Curly, itching for a good scrap. "There's a bunch of baboons pickin' on the bushmen!!! Git that there pachyderm a snortful of water and climb aboard!"

Birds flutter from trees! Animals scatter wildly in all directions! The entire Serengeti trembles as the mighty Tanzanian elephant tree thunders down on the bushmen's brouhaha!

One blast from Buffy's massive honker douses the fire and sends the terrified blue-nosed baboons scrambling into the surrounding savannah.

With the brouhaha quelled, the Bungalo Boys head back to base camp Bravo Bravo. It has been a long day of adventure, and the boys look forward to some early shut-eye. Morning will come soon, and they have only begun to unravel the secrets of the Serengeti!

The Bungalo Boys III
By John Bianchi
Champions of Hockey

The swoosh of steel on ice. The clatter of stick and puck.
Sounds that crackle through frosted morning air. Sounds of the Bungalo
Boys preparing for competition—a contest of skill, strength, grace and
pluck. Sounds of hockey—the world's fastest game!

At stake is the symbol of hockey supremacy — the Bungalo Birdbath, installed by Great-Great-Granduncle Guido de Bungalo in 1889. Family tradition plays a big part in all Birdbath games. For 99 years, the Bath has been successfully defended against all challengers by the Bungalo sports dynasty. Indeed, many feel that the ghosts of these great hockey legends haunt the beaver pond to this very day.

This year's challengers are a mystery team from the Natural Hockey League. As player-coach Ma Bungalo puts her boys through their pregame skate, anxious eyes search the visitors' end of the ice. Finally, three small figures appear.

"It's a bunch of penguins!" laughs Curly. The rest of the boys cannot resist a moment of mirth. But their laughter is short-lived. Out of the morning haze, like three great ocean tankers clearing a fog, lumbers the rest of the NHL's team . . .

. . . the Bruins.

The icy determination that once flowed through the boys' veins quickly turns to Zamboni slush.

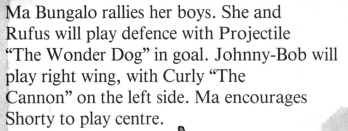

Ma Bungalo rallies her boys. She and Rufus will play defence with Projectile "The Wonder Dog" in goal. Johnny-Bob will play right wing, with Curly "The Cannon" on the left side. Ma encourages Shorty to play centre.

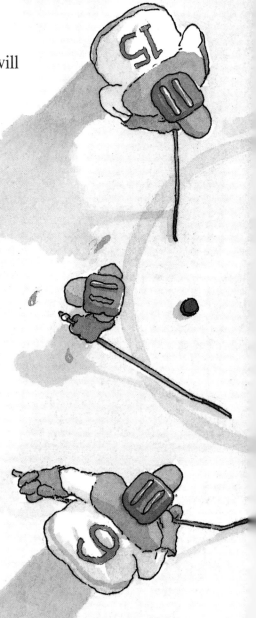

The NHL counters with its famous "Bird" line. The Bruins will play defence. All agree to use the honour system and call their own penalties.

The boys get off to a slow start. Little Shorty plays giveaway in his own end, and one of the big Bruin defencebears easily converts the miscue. NHL: one. Bungalos: no score.

Then, after going down to block a shot, Little Shorty coughs up the puck. Projectile is helpless as one of the Penguins wastes no time turning on the red light. NHL: two. Bungalos: no score.

Midway through the second period, Little Shorty takes a costly penalty and quickly sends himself to the penalty box. Inspired by the loss of their little centre, the Bungalos capitalize on their one-man disadvantage and score two unanswered goals. NHL: two. Bungalos: two.

In the third period, the NHL launches an all-out attack. The team pulls its big bruin goalie and fore-checks the Bungalos into their own end. The beaver pond has never seen such heavy action!

Suddenly, with a sickening **"CA-SPLASH,"** the ice shatters!

Out of the mayhem drifts a lone skater with the puck.
Little Shorty has a breakaway!

During the post-game celebrations, the Bungalo Boys
congratulate each other on a game well played.
"We're still number one!" roars Curly.
"We never gave up!" shouts Johnny-Bob.
"We just did what we had to do!" cries Rufus.
"It was 60 minutes of teamwork," notes Ma.
"Cause we're the Champions of Hockey!" they all scream.
"And best of all," adds Little Shorty with relief,
"no one got into a fight."